D0634742

9112000276071

For every child who dares to be different,
and for Mel and Rob, with love – S.P-H.

For my students – K.M.

Text copyright © Smriti Prasadam-Halls 2015
Illustrations copyright © Katherina Manolessou 2015

The right of Smriti Prasadam-Halls to be identified as the author and Katherina Manolessou to be identified
as the illustrator of this work has been asserted in accordance with the Copyright, Designs and
Patents Act, 1988 (United Kingdom).

First published in Great Britain in 2015 by Frances Lincoln Children's Books.
This paperback edition first published in Great Britain in 2016 by Frances Lincoln Children's Books,
74-77 White Lion Street, London N1 9PF
www.franceslincoln.com

A catalogue record for this book is available from the British Library.

ISBN 978-1-84780-684-0

The illustrations are screenprinted

Printed in China

1 3 5 7 9 8 6 4 2

T-Veg

The story of a carrot-crunching dinosaur

Smriti Prasadam-Halls

Illustrated by
Katherina Manolessou

Frances Lincoln
Children's Books

Reginald the T-rex had
a fierce and mighty
ROAR!

His fierce and mighty
footsteps thundered through
the jungle floor.

He ran as fast
and leapt as far
as any T-rex could.

He stomped about
and GNASHED
his teeth as every T-rex should.

He just had one small worry,
one teeny, tiny thing...
At dinner-time he often felt
that he did not fit in.

For while the other T-rexes
munched on juicy steak...

...Reginald the T-rex ate crunchy

CARROT CAKE!

Reginald ate BROCCOLI, Reginald ate BEANS.
Reginald ate bowls and bowls of GARLIC, GRAPES and GREENS.

"It's just so yum!" he told his friends. "You must give this a try," while wolfing down a massive slice of AVOCADO pie.

MANGOES, PEACHES, PINEAPPLES, he ate them by the dish.

"BANANA-BERRY shake," he'd say. "Mmm, that's SO delish!"

CARROTS, PARSNIPS, LETTUCES... oh yes, he ate them too!
And for a tea-time treat he munched on pea and spinach stew.

"For goodness sake what's wrong with you?"

Papa T-rex groaned.

"You should be eating

MEAT,

MEAT,

MEAT!"

Mama T-rex moaned.

"You'll never win the Tyrannolympics!"
laughed his best friend Hugh.

"Why ever not?" asked Reginald. "I'm just as FAST as you."

At school the others all poked fun. They didn't understand.
"There's never been a vegetarian T-rex in this land!"

"T-rexes need lots of meat,
it's THAT that makes us strong.
And if you're eating vegetables,
you're doing it ALL WRONG!"

"Ho ho ho," and "Ha, ha, ha," they laughed at poor old Reg.
"You're not a T-rex after all...
Tyrannosaurus VEG!"

So, feeling rather miserable, Reg packed his dino-sack.
"Goodbye! I'm leaving home," he called, "and NEVER coming back!"

"I want to find some better friends who'll understand me more.
The truth might be that actually I am a HERBIVORE!
I'll try and do some herbie things. It will be FUN I bet...

But standing deep in river slime was
HORRID,
COLD
and WET!

He tried to do some MOOING but it sounded just like roaring,

and slowing to a gentle jog was just a little BORING.

And when it came to FORAGING, Reg didn't have a clue.
"I'd better find some herbivores to show me what to do!"

"What luck!" cried Reg. A group of them were grazing just ahead.
He started stomping faster. "I'll make friends with THEM," he said.
But as he charged to greet them and was still quite far away...

The herbies took one look at Reg...

and **SHRIEKED**

and **RAN AWAY!**

Meanwhile at home the T-rexes were missing T-rex Reg.
"So what if he ate fruit?" said Hugh. "So what if he ate veg?
There's no one who can stomp like him, or play our T-rex games.
We HAVE to go and find him quick and bring him home again."

Off they set but pretty soon they heard a distant rumble.
The clifftop right above their heads began to
creak... **creak**... **crumble**.

A MASSIVE rock was slowly crash...

crash...
CRASHING

down the hill.

The T-rex clan was sure they
would be crushed, that was, UNTIL...

Reginald the T-rex spotted them from far away.

He galloped to their rescue and he bravely saved the day!

He pushed with all his might and stopped the boulder with his weight.

He held it back and set them free before it was too late.

The T-rex crew were so amazed.

"Hurrah for **T-VEG REG!**
You're just so **STRONG!**"

"Oh yes," Reg laughed.
"It's all my
FRUIT and VEG!"

"CARROTS help me see," he said. "BANANAS give me speed
and PEAS and SPINACH help to give me all the strength I need.
So though I might eat vegetables it doesn't mean I'm weak."

"Of course you're not,"
said all the rest.
"You're strong and you're
unique!"

"Now please say you'll come home again
and make our herd complete."
"I will," said Reg, "as long as you don't
laugh at what I eat."
"We never will again!" declared the
sorry T-rex crew.
"And if you give us one more chance,
we'll make it up to you."

And so the dinos cooked a FEAST of vegetable kebabs,
and roasted squash and mushrooms
which they all agreed were FAB!

And then they danced the night away,
because they KNOW it's true...
the best thing in the world is being happy being YOU!